Enid Blyton ™
The Tale of the Blue-Eyed Cat

Illustrated by Pam Storey

Copyright and trademarks are the property of Enid Blyton Ltd.
All rights reserved.
Illustrations copyright © 1997 Grandreams Ltd
This edition published 2002
© Robert Frederick Ltd.,4 North Parade, Bath
Printed in China

“I wish,” said the black cat loudly, “I do wish that the pink rabbit would go to some other toy cupboard to live.”

The black cat was a toy cat. She wasn't much bigger than a small kitten, but she was as grown-up as a cat in her ways.

The pink rabbit glared at the toy cat. “And I wish,” he said, “that the silly black cat with blue eyes would go jump out of the window. Blue eyes! Whoever heard of blue eyes for a cat? Cats have green ones.”

"Now, now," said the teddy bear. "Don't start squabbling again, you two. You really ought to behave better, Rabbit, because you are much older than the toy cat."

The pink rabbit scowled. He was dressed very smartly in blue velvet trousers and a red coat. On his coat were three glass buttons, as green as grass. The pink rabbit was very proud of them.

"Look!" he said to the cat, pointing to his gleaming buttons. "Why haven't you got eyes as green as my buttons? Fancy having blue eyes!"

"Be quiet, Rabbit. She can't help it," said the big doll. "I've got blue eyes, too."

"It's nice in a doll," said the rabbit. "And look at that cat's tail, too – all the hairs have come off at the end!"

"Well, she couldn't help the puppy chewing her tail," said the bear. "Don't be so mean and bad-tempered, Rabbit."

That was the worst of Rabbit. He was so mean. If anyone did anything he didn't like, he said mean things and played nasty tricks, too, on anybody that had annoyed him. When the bear grumbled at him one day, he hid behind the curtain with a big pin. And as soon as the bear came along, Rabbit pinned him to the curtain so that he couldn't get away. That was the sort of thing he did.

So nobody liked him much, and they all thought him vain and silly.

The black cat disliked him very much. If she could she would always turn her back on him, and he didn't like that.

"Stuck-up creature!" he grumbled. "With her silly blue ribbon and great, staring blue eyes."

One day the toy cat found a piece of chocolate dropped on the floor. She was very pleased. She bit it into many small pieces, and gave a bit to all her friends. But she didn't give even a lick to the rabbit.

"Mean thing!" he said, when he saw everyone munching chocolate. "All right; you just wait. I'll pay you back some day, yes, I will!"

Now, the next week, the black cat felt worried. She couldn't see properly out of one of her blue eyes. She told the bear about it and he had a look at the eye.

"Goodness! It's coming loose!" he said. "I hope Mary notices it, Cat, or it may drop off and be lost. You'd look funny with only one eye."

Mary was the little girl in whose playroom they all lived. The toy cat kept staring at her, hoping she would notice her loose eye. But she didn't.

Mary had just got a new book and she couldn't stop reading it. You know how it is when you want to go on reading.

So the toy's cat got looser and looser. At last it was hanging on by only one thread, and still Mary hadn't noticed it. She was nearly at the end of her book, though, and the cat hoped that maybe her eye would hold on till Mary had finished reading. Then she would be sure to notice her poor toy cat's eye.

But that night, after Mary had gone to bed, the cat's eye dropped right off! She had been sitting quite still, afraid she might jerk it off – and then she had forgotten to keep still and had run across the room to speak to the bear.

She felt her eye falling out. It fell on the floor with a thud – and then it rolled away under the couch! The cat gave a cry.

"Oh, my eye's gone! It's under the couch. Please get it, somebody!"

The toys all lay down and peeped under the couch. All except the rabbit. He wasn't going to bother himself! But suddenly he saw, quite near his foot, something that shone blue. He stared at it. Gracious, it was the toy cat's eye! It must have rolled under the couch and out the other side, and have come right over to where the rabbit sat looking at a picture book!

He looked at the other toys. They were all poking about under the couch. The toy cat was watching, crying tears out of her one eye.

Quick as lightning the rabbit put his foot over the blue glass eye. He kicked it into a corner. Then he got up, went to the corner and, without anybody noticing, put the eye into his pocket.

"Now I've got the cat's eye!" he thought. "Good! She won't get it back again, that's for certain. I'll pay her back now for all the things she said to me."

He went over to the toys and pretended to look for the eye with them. But all the time he could feel it in his pocket. He wanted to laugh.

"Perhaps I'd better hide it safely somewhere," he thought suddenly. "If any of the toys found out that I had the eye, I should get into dreadful trouble. They might turn me out of the playroom. Now, where can I put it?"

Well, you will never guess where he hid it! It really was a very clever place. He went into the dolls' house. There was nobody there, for all the dolls were helping the cat to look for her dropped eye.

He went into the kitchen. He lifted up the lid of the tiny kettle set on the toy stove – and he dropped the eye in there. It just went in nicely. Then he put the lid on and ran out quietly. Nobody would ever, ever find the eye now, because the dolls' house dolls never used that kettle. They had a smaller one they liked better.

The toy cat was very miserable indeed. She cried bitterly. The toys tried to comfort her. Only the pink rabbit didn't say anything nice. He was glad.

"How mean and unkind you are, Rabbit," said everyone.

But he didn't care a bit.

The next day Mary finished her book and had time to look at her toys again. And, of course, she noticed at once that the toy cat had only one eye. She was very upset.

"You look dreadful!" she said. "You must have dropped it. I'll look around for it." But she couldn't find it, of course, because it was in the kettle.

"Whatever shall I do with you?" said Mary to the miserable toy cat. "You can't go about with one eye, that's for certain. And I haven't got a blue button that would do for you. What can I do?"

She looked at all the other toys and she suddenly saw the pink rabbit, dressed so smartly in his velvet coat and trousers, with the three gleaming green buttons on his coat.

"Oh! Of course! I know what to do," cried Mary, and she picked up the surprised rabbit. "You can have two new eyes, Toy Cat – proper green ones, this time! I'll take off your old blue one and put on two of these beautiful green ones. You will look simply lovely!"

Well, what do you think of that? Snip, snip went Mary's scissors and, to the pink rabbit's horror, the two top buttons of his coat fell off.

Then Mary took the one blue eye off the cat and put on the two green ones instead. You can't imagine how handsome the cat looked, with two green eyes instead of blue ones. She stared round at the toys in delight.

The toy cat looked lovely but the pink rabbit felt cross and unhappy. He had lost his beautiful green buttons and that awful cat had got them instead. She was looking at him with his own buttons for eyes. The rabbit could hardly stop himself from crying with rage.

Now, the toys might have been sorry for the rabbit, and tried to comfort him, if something else hadn't happened just then. Mary suddenly decided to give a party for the toy cat to celebrate her beautiful new eyes. She took the kettle off the toy stove to fill with water.

And inside she found the blue eye of the toy cat! She picked it out of the kettle in great aston-ishment. She looked at it, and so did all the toys.

"Who ever put that there?" said Mary.

Nobody said anything. But something strange happened to the rabbit's pink face. It turned a dark red. Everyone stared at him in surprise, and then they knew who had hidden the eye. It was the naughty pink rabbit!

"So you hid it!" said Mary. "You naughty, mean toy. I suppose you think I'm going to take off the toy cat's green eyes and give them back to you as buttons now that we have two blue eyes for her again. But I'm not. She can keep her green eyes now. She looks very beautiful with them. As for you, it was a very good punishment to lose your lovely buttons. And, what is more, you shan't come to the party."

"Oh, let him come," said the toy cat, so happy now because she had such beautiful green eyes that she simply couldn't be unkind to anyone. "Let him come. I'll forgive him. Give him a chance to be nice."

So he came. But he was very quiet and sad and well-behaved.

The toys all think he may be better now. But he does feel strange when he feels the toy cat staring at him through buttons he once wore on his coat!

Enid Blyton™
The Beautiful Pattern

Illustrated by Pam Storey

Copyright and trademarks are the property of Enid Blyton Ltd.
All rights reserved.
Illustrations copyright © 1997 Grandreams Ltd
This edition published 2002
© Robert Frederick Ltd., 4 North Parade, Bath
Printed in China

Once upon a time there was a little boy called Morris. He went to school and he was very good at all his lessons – except drawing. You should have seen the pictures he drew!

"Well, really, Morris, I don't know if this drawing is meant to be a dustbin, a house, an elephant or a banana!" his teacher said one day. "And this is the best pattern you can make for me? Well, I really do think you might have done better than this!"

The children often drew patterns in the drawing-lesson and coloured the patterns they made. Sometimes they were quite simple ones, like this:

or prettier ones like this:

They could draw what patterns they liked, and they could use the letters of the alphabet or figures or anything they pleased, so long as they made a really pretty pattern. It was fun to chalk the patterns.

Poor Morris could never think of a good pattern at all. Once he thought it would be a good thing to do a pattern of aeroplanes, but when he drew them they looked rather like birds with no head and two tails – so it wasn't such a good pattern after all.

One day the teacher gave her children some homework to do over the weekend.

"I want you to think of a really lovely pattern," she said, "the sort of pattern that would look nice on our wallpaper.

Now do think of an unusual and beautiful one, draw it out on a sheet of paper and then colour it."

Poor Morris! When he got home and sat down with his sheet of paper and a pencil, do you suppose he could think of any pattern at all? Not one!

I expect you could think of plenty and draw them beautifully – but you are cleverer than Morris.

"It's a shame!" thought Morris, leaning his head on his hand. "I can do sums well, and I'm always top in history – but I just CAN'T draw!"

"Morris! Whatever are you looking so worried about?" called his mother. "Don't sit and look so gloomy. Put on your hat and coat and go out into the snow. The sun is shining and it will do you good to go and play."

So Morris put on his hat and coat and out he went into the snow. He thought he would go to the little wood nearby. It was a lovely place, because the trees grew very close together and made it rather exciting and mysterious.

Off he went and into the little wood. And there he saw something he had never seen before. It was a little house made of snow! It had snow walls, a snow chimney, windows made of little sheets of ice, and no door at all – just an opening.

"What a dear little house!" thought Morris. "I wonder who made it? Surely no one can live there?"

He went to the house. He peeped in at the window, but he could see nothing through the ice-panes. He went to the doorway and peeped through the opening.

And inside he saw a long-bearded brownie, very busy papering the snow walls of his house!

"Good gracious!" said Morris. "Are you really a brownie? I didn't think you lived anywhere except in books! Are you real?"

"Well, what a question to ask anyone!" said the brownie crossly. "What a funny boy you are! Do you think I'm a dream, or something?"

"Well, you might be," said Morris. "I say – what a lovely wallpaper! Where did you get it from?"

"I made it myself," said the brownie. "I did the pattern myself too. Do you like it?"

"It's a marvellous pattern," said Morris, looking at it. "How did you think of it? I can never think of patterns like this."

"Oh, I don't think of them," said the brownie, his green eyes shining as he looked at Morris. "I just go out and look for them!"

"Look for patterns!" cried Morris. "Well, I wish I could do that! I'm always getting into trouble at school because I can't do patterns. Where do you see your patterns when you go to look for them?"

"Well, last summer I made a beautiful pattern of daisy-heads," said the brownie. "Quite easy too, it was – just a little round middle with petals all round it. I made a most beautiful wallpaper of that. And another time I went out into the woods and found some green bracken just beginning to grow and to uncurl its green fingers – and I made a pattern of that too."

"What lovely things to make patterns from!" said Morris. "But this wallpaper of yours hasn't daisies or bracken on. It's not a flower pattern at all. What is it? I'm sure you've made it up!"

"No, I haven't," said the brownie. "I got this pattern from the snow."

Morris stared at him in surprise. "But I've never seen the snow in patterns like that!" he said.

"Ah, that's because you haven't looked carefully enough at the snow-crystals," said the brownie. "Each snow-crystal is a little pattern in itself – didn't you know that?"

"No, I didn't," said Morris. "I don't even know what you mean."

"Whatever do they teach you at school?" said the brownie, in astonishment. "Why, at the brownie school I went to we all learnt about the beauty of snow-crystals. Well, I'll tell you. You've seen snowflakes falling, haven't you?"

"Of course," said Morris. "They are falling again now."

"Well, each snowflake is made up of snow-crystals," said the brownie. "And now, here is a funny thing – every snow-crystal is different, and yet it is the same in one thing – it is six-sided! Shall we go and catch some snowflakes and look at them through my magic glass? Then you will see what I mean."

11

So out they went into the wood, where the snow was beginning to fall quite thickly. The little brownie took with him a piece of black velvet and he caught a snowflake on this. Then he took out a round glass in a frame and made Morris look at the snowflake through the glass – and to the boy's great surprise he saw that the flake was made up of snow-crystals lightly joined together and every single crystal had six sides to it! Not one of them had four sides or five sides or seven sides – each had six. They were all quite different, but they were very beautiful.

"How perfectly lovely!" said Morris, astonished. "Oh, I do like them! Look – here is one rather like the pattern on your wallpaper! No wonder you managed to get such a pretty pattern, brownie – why, there are dozens of different patterns for you to use in one snowflake!"

"Yes," said the brownie. "I chose one the other day and drew it out on my paper, then coloured it. Don't you think it will look sweet on the walls of my new snow-house?"

"I do," said Morris. "You've given me such a good idea, brownie! I'm going straight home now to make a snow-crystal pattern. That's my homework this weekend. I ought to get top marks, for I am sure no one else will have such a lovely pattern as mine!"

"Well, good-bye," said the brownie, going back into his house. "I must go on with my papering. Come back on Monday afternoon and tell me if you got top marks."

Morris ran home. He burst into the sitting-room and told his mother all about the brownie and his magic glass. "I wish I had asked him to lend it to me," he said. "Then I could have chosen the prettiest snow-crystal to do. I'm afraid I shan't remember one very well."

"I have a kind of magic glass you can see through," said his mother. "It's Daddy's magnifying glass! It makes things look much bigger when you look through it. I'll get it."

She fetched it and Morris went outside to catch a snowflake on his coat-sleeve and looked at it through the magnifying glass. Goodness, how lovely the six-sided crystals were! Like stars or flowers, very small and perfect.

"I'll make a pattern just like that one there," said Morris to himself, and he looked at the crystal very carefully indeed to get it into his memory. Then he went indoors and got his sheet of paper. He drew a row of six-sided crystals, then another and another and another, till he had a whole page of them. Then he coloured them beautifully and took his pattern to his mother.

"How marvellous!" she cried. "This is the loveliest pattern you have ever done! How I would like to have it for my wallpaper!"

Well, as you can guess, Morris got top marks for it and the teacher pinned the pattern up on the wall for everyone to see. Morris could hardly wait for the afternoon to come, because he so badly wanted to tell the brownie that he had done a beautiful snow-crystal and got top marks!

He looked out of the window. The sun was shining brightly and felt quite hot on his hand.

Morris rushed off to the wood as soon as he could – but oh, what a disappointment! The sun had melted the snow and there was no little snow-house to be seen! There was only a wet pile of paper on which Morris could just see the pattern the brownie had made.

"His wallpaper!" thought Morris. "Poor little brownie! His house didn't last long. Well, he did me a good turn, no doubt about that! I shall know where to get my patterns from now – I shall look about in the fields and woods for them!"

Would you like to make a pattern of six-sided snow-crystals? Well, catch a snowflake on something dark and look at it through a magnifying glass! You will see what Morris and the brownie saw – dainty six-sided crystals, all different and all beautiful!